BETH BALL

HEXBLADE

FEATHER & FLAME NOVELLA

Published by Grove Guardian Press

Edited by Kat Betts of Element Editing Services

Cover design by Mibl Art

Paperback ISBN 978-1-952609-44-2

Ebook ISBN 978-1-952609-43-5

groveguardianpress.com

ALSO BY BETH BALL

Feather & Flame

Phoenix Rising

From the Ashes (forthcoming)

Age of Azuria

Buried Heroes

Hadvarian Heist

Amber Queen

Forest Deep

Shadows Beneath

Heir of Lilith Trilogy

Phantom

Pain (forthcoming)

Novellas and Short Stories

Hexblade, a *Feather & Flame* novella

"Awakened Flame," an *Age of Azuria* story

Aurora, an *Age of Azuria* novella

Song of Parting, an *Age of Azuria* novella

Story Magic, an *Age of Azuria* novella

Stormborn, a standalone *Tree of Silver* novella

Promise, an *Heir of Lilith* novella

DUR'FOR
HALLOWED
HILLS
BASTIO
VERITA
THE GLADE OF SHADOWS
SCOURGE

NORTHLANDS
FAER HAVEN
VESTIGE
SANCTUARY
MERIDIENNE MOUNTAINS
RESPITE
IS-MAEN
RCLE
THE GREEN MOUNTAINS
THE EMERAUDE
PALAIS
BEACON
THE WORLD OF ELDURA

CHAPTER ONE

THE SORCERESS

ACADEMIA MAGICA, DELMOIR, LIS-MAEN

From high in her tower upon the academy grounds, the Sorceress held aside the velvet curtains that separated her from a view of the city of Delmoir that stretched below. The academy had long been the seat of power where the traditions of natural magic gathered, with the most resistant tradition, that of the druids, having yielded its former insistence of separation and joining their line to that of the other Faces a few decades before. Much had changed within the Academia Magica in the decades since she and the other Faces had brought the Druidess to dwell among them, but the gardens of Delmoir had never looked better.

A knock sounded upon her door.

"Enter."

She'd been waiting for this moment since first spying the airship over the bay of the Circle Sea beyond

Delmoir. It had been a calculated risk, exposing her interest in the workings of their rivals and near-enemies, the forces of the Cities United through so obvious a means of transportation for her agent, but the Cities' generals already suspected she was watching over their movements.

The Sorceress knew they were surveying hers—she'd had three of her apprentices turned over to the experimenters in the last fortnight for suspected spying. They could not prove their innocence, so she found a different way for them to lend their worth to the greater cause.

The door to her study creaked open, and a breathless scout appeared. The slanted evening sun was low enough to allow her reflection upon the glass. Through the panes, the Sorceress met her scout's eyes. "Tell me."

"It is only a matter of hours now, perhaps days, until Sanctuary passes into Her clutches. The Cities will be weakened. Desperate."

The Sorceress smiled. She had been waiting for the Cities' defenses to crumble. It was really only a matter of time before one of the cities bowed to the will of the dark goddess. Sanctuary was the next in a logical line of destruction—an outcome she was determined to protect Lis-Maen from.

"You have done well." She brushed her hand through the air, dismissing one who might prove dedicated and skilled enough to one day be among her protégés. "Send for the Oracle." Of the other four Faces beyond herself, the Oracle was the most forward minded.

The Sorceress nearly smirked—their situation would have been far more dire were that not the case. But what she needed in an ally was one with an iron stomach. One who would perceive what had to be done.

Her scout thanked her for her generosity and did as the Sorceress bid.

The Sorceress strode away from the window, pacing across her office to the large desk she kept at its center with maps and pages strewn across.

There at the crux of the map of Eldura—the heart of their world, was the island of Lis-Maen, with Delmoir, their capital, at its northeastern coast. Across their northern borders were the territories of the Cities United, separated by the Circle Sea. To the southeast stretched the vast forests of the Emeraude, the domain of the witches—sisters in magic and spirit, though unaffiliated with the Five Faces of the Pentacle: herself, the Creatrix, the Oracle, the Healer, and now the Druidess.

Southwest of Lis-Maen was the domain of the dark goddess Alessandra, the continent of Scourge. And bordering it to their west was the Glade of Shadows, the realm of the dryads, independent bands of fae, and the elusive Sapphire Circle, a powerful and reclusive druid conclave that held itself apart from the border conclaves across Lis-Maen.

She ticked her tongue behind her teeth, scanning the reports. *Desperate*, she repeated to herself, thumping shut the ledger she kept of experiments. The names of the three apprentices had been crossed through. Even she was not so profane as to continue her experiments beyond death. Well, at least not usually.

Sanctuary lingered at the edge of the Cities United, with the city of Vestige beyond it. It was a puzzling move for the dark goddess Alessandra to make, seizing a city on the opposite side of their world from her strongholds across Scourge, the territory she had ruled without question for the better part of a millennium.

The ghost of a smile twisted into a smirk—seizing Sanctuary would cut off the Cities' military jewel, Respite, from easy passage to Vestige, and it made the self-righteous city of Beacon even more isolated than it had been before. The dark goddess's army would be one mountain range away from the center of the Cities' holdings in Respite.

With that perspective, it was a wonder the city had stood for so long. With it, Alessandra functionally bifurcated the concentrated might of the Cities United, and such a move weakened some of the pressure placed upon Lis-Maen, their small island nation at the center of the war between the Cities and Alessandra.

She ran her tongue over her teeth. The dark goddess's maneuver, if Sanctuary were to fall, *could* make their holdings in Lis-Maen more vulnerable. If Alessandra wanted to press her advantage, cut off Respite from seafaring routes, strangle its trade—

A second knock interrupted her musings, and the Oracle strode through the door. "You called for me?"

The Sorceress narrowed her gaze as she surveyed the most practical and far-sighted of her fellow Faces, though such a distinction was not overly impressive considering the antiquated ideals of the Healer and Creatrix. They were five in total, the Pentacle, and though none of them were her equal in mind or might, she had to start somewhere.

"My scouts tell me that Sanctuary is about to fall." She held the Oracle's gaze. Like herself, her fellow Face was skilled at masking her emotions, but this was not the time for caution. It was the time for decisive action. "What do you say to that, Sister?"

Mysteries shone behind the Oracle's eyes with the delicate wrinkles at their corners deepening ever so slightly. Often while she waited for the Seer to speak, the Sorceress found herself remembering that she was staring into the very same shining orbs the Oracle's daughter would consume to carry on the magic and wisdom of their line. A barbarous practice. Disgusting.

The lineage of the Sorceress was far more refined—she had poisoned her mentor and claimed her grimoire for her own. If one of her protégés had the wisdom and tenacity to do the same to her then so be it. Unfortunately for them, they usually perished while attempting a magic that was beyond them in order to impress her or, if one truly became a threat, in a magical trial she challenged them to that they subsequently failed. She had watched her mentor do the same. As had been true in her own days as a protégé, they were just as deadly to one another as they might one day be to her. Still, preferable to plucking out and devouring your mother's eyes.

"I see one of two ways forward," the Oracle began. As was often her habit, her hand hovered before her body, as though she was trying to feel her way through a dense fog. "In the first, we attempt to revive the magic of Verdigris across our island—it is why we allowed the Druidess with her inferior magic into our midst, after all. Or"—

her hazel eyes flashed, promising violence—"we begin our reclamation of what the Cities took from us."

A slow smile spread across the Sorceress's face. She had been right to entrust the scout's report to the Oracle. It was a cunning aim indeed to revive the lost magic of the Titan of Nature. Cunning, too, to press their advantage and their quest for revenge and independence during the Cities' time of weakness and divided attention. In this matter, as with the courting of the Druidess decades before, their minds were of one accord. "And when we reclaim the pure elemental magic for ourselves," she answered, "we create an unconquerable, weaponized force."

"A perfect weapon," the Oracle added.

The Sorceress's fingertips prickled at the thought. A cadre of mages specifically trained to bear the pure energy of the elements could repel any incursion the Cities sent their way. Lis-Maen could truly be independent from the Cities' warmongering. And with so powerful an offering, they might even have equal footing upon which to propose an arrangement with the dark goddess. What could it hurt to keep their options truly open?

Arcana Suya Tu—the ancient motto of the Sorceress's line. *Magical knowledge over all else.*

She would see their legacy through better than any predecessor. And with such a feat, with such an offering to be made to Alessandra, she could find a way to maintain her position eternally.

"We will need to acquire some of their alchemists," the Sorceress mused, affecting a casual tone. She doubted that the Oracle would believe she'd only just thought of this eventuality, but pretending gave them both plausible deniability until such precautions were no longer necessary.

The Oracle nodded. "A wise precaution to ensure the safety of our own efforts."

"Precisely." The Sorceress drummed her nails against the polished wood of her desk. "I believe they'll be more comfortable if their families come along as well."

Her colleague bowed. "I will see it done." With no further need for discussion between them for the moment, the Oracle brushed the long tail of her coat aside and strode toward the door.

She paused at the threshold. "At what point should we inform the others?"

The Sorceress pursed her lips. She had been considering this as well. "When the first round of offerings is ready." It was harder to keep her tone neutral this time. The cluelessness of the elder Faces was nothing short of humorous. A most unfortunate trait for those trapped beneath them but, truth be told, if their underlings could have risen in the superior magic of sorcery, they wouldn't be in this predicament. "They should do their part."

"Understood," the Oracle said before gliding into the hall.

Alone in her study once more, the Sorceress returned her gaze to the map of Eldura spread before her. She pressed the poisoned tip of her nail into Sanctuary, piercing the parchment. *The first to fall.*

It would only be a matter of time until the other

Cities followed. And in their wake, Lis-Maen would rise to the position of prominence it deserved.

It would only naturally follow that the one who had brought such a chance into being would be promoted to sole rulership at that time. Sorceress Eterna, they would call her. Right-hand of the dark goddess, and the most powerful mage Eldura had ever seen.

CHAPTER TWO

THE ORACLE

The Oracle smoothed the front tails of her coat as she strolled out of the Sorceress's tower room, taking care to not appear in a rush.

In contrast to her deliberate strides, her mind raced ahead. A letter warning Yvayne and a separate one to Kailena were already composing themselves in her mind.

The Sorceress made no secret of her fear of the druids of the interior in her blatant disdain for the Druidess, as though the druids' magic did not enliven the whole of Lis-Maen and make the magic of the other four Faces possible.

The relocation of the hearttrees, save one, from the forests to the Sacred Grove outside the Pentacle had been too cleverly executed for any of them to stop it, but they would need to get ahead of the Sorceress's perfect-weapon scheme lest she use it to eliminate all but the most unpromising of bloodlines from Lis-Maen's interior.

"I am not to be disturbed," she instructed her guards as she returned to her rooms.

The two women nodded, unsheathing their scimitars from their scabbards and stepping in front of her double oak doors as the Oracle shut herself inside. Yvayne would see to warning their allies in the Emeraude of the Sorceress's growing ambitions. The Sapphire Circle and the dryads in the Glade of Shadows as well.

She could not afford to be so profuse in her correspondence as it was closely monitored by the Sorceress and her spies, not to mention those who bore the Pentacle and the Academia Magica ill will from both the forces of the Cities United and those of the dark goddess.

Her allies in Vestige were currently deployed at the front in Sanctuary, guided by Camelia's Sight. The Seer would guide them through whatever trials they faced at Alessandra's hands, but now was not the time to press new troubles upon her head. There were a few saudad lingering near Yvayne's hideout in the Emeraude. She would leave it to the fae to determine whether or not to bring them into their fold.

She unfurled a parchment scroll upon her desk and prepared to write her missive when a puff of rosemary from her incense in the corner whispered through her nose. A call to wisdom.

The Oracle returned her quill to its stand and stoppered the inkwell.

The air spirits were right—she would seek the wisdom of the Old Ones through the beads before proceeding.

Perhaps they had more to show her yet.

She rose from her desk and slipped her coat from her shoulders, placing it and her belt of throwing knives over the back of her chair. Already she felt lighter, the worn linen of her tunic and breeches allowing the first flutters of the evening breeze to trail through the fabric and against her skin.

On the far side of her office was the door to her sanctum. Each of the Faces had a sacred room of this sort, though the nuances of the room changed depending on the mage's personal practice and the norms of their magical line.

The Healer's room was filled with tinctures and records. The Creatrix's raw materials—crystals and herbs. The Druidess kept a veritable greenhouse in hers filled with woodland critters and songbirds. Predictably, the Sorceress never allowed anyone into her room, but in the one glimpse the Oracle had caught of it in their decades working together, she'd seen two windows— one for the sun and a larger one for the moons, both of which would shine down upon a pedestal in the center of the room upon which rested a single book.

The Oracle had only made a few changes to her mother's room when she inherited the mantle of their line.

Her stomach had still been unsettled from the Ceremony of Eyes when she stepped into the room for the first time.

The room had been built within an open-air terrace in the earliest generations of the Academia Magica's founding. One of her ancestors had added layered glass panes to the terrace, walling it in so that the Oracle could consult the beads without being visible to those beyond the tower while still allowing in the light. The tallest five feet of the walled-in tower had been left open to permit the wind and rain their say over the beads as well.

She shut the glass door behind herself and lit the censer in the corner. The Oracle closed her eyes and stood within the incense smoke, allowing it to clear away the energetic remnants of the Sorceress's ambition so it would not cloud her understanding of the beads' message.

When her mind was clear, she approached the wall of wooden beads in the center of the room. They rattled as she neared, dancing between her energy and the gusts of wind flickering down from the gaps overhead.

She ran her hands along the beaded wall. Runes had been carved into the beads' surfaces to enable readings. The wooden cylinders clicked beneath her fingers as they had for generations of her ancestors.

Beneath the spinning beads lay the many twisting possibilities of fate, the countless iterations of what might be. Her responsibility—following after her mother, her mother's mother, her grandmother's mother, and so on, back for more than one thousand years—was to discern what the next right possibility of fate was, particularly given the clashing ambitions of their allies and enemies alike. What would best serve the myriad peoples of Lis-Maen? Renew the druids' faith in their magic, slake the Sorceress's thirst for power?

The Oracle shut her eyes. What course would best serve her daughter, and her daughter's daughter, across the generations after her?

Through the black and blood-thrum of her eyelids, a wide-winged phoenix slid through the invisible currents of the vast woodland of her imagination. The beads spun without the urging of her fingers. The Oracle inhaled a sharp breath.

It couldn't be.

Behind the closed eyes of her mind, the phoenix descended from the skies. As she landed upon the leaf-ridden forest floor, her wings collapsed in at her sides. The phoenix raised her regal head, and she transformed from bird into woman, with flowing hair and pointed ears. The markings of each of the six elements glowed about her—the sacred signature of Verdigris, the lost titan.

Here is your answer, the whirring beads spun to say. *Unite the six, and a wandering soul will return. In her wake, for good and ill, many destinies will be fulfilled.*

The Oracle stumbled away from the wall, resting her hand against the chill of the glass instead.

The Sorceress should be allowed to proceed, the beads had said.

And the sign they'd been waiting for had arrived.

The Oracle shivered and rubbed her arms, trying to dispel the goosebumps that had risen across her skin. It was the clearest vision her ancestors had ever granted to her.

She slipped through the glass doorway and rushed back to her desk. Yvayne and Kailena had to know of this.

The sign of Lilia appeared to me.

It is time for the granddaughter of Verdigris to return, she wrote.

"Mama?" Her daughter's voice caught her off-guard, and the Oracle jumped, smearing the wet ink of her letter to Yvayne.

"What is it, light of my eyes?" The Oracle cleared her throat, conscious of the warble in her voice.

Her daughter, fully grown into her elf ears and figure now, peered at her strangely.

The Oracle's mother had always addressed her in the pet name that promised what was to come, though she had not used it for her own daughter for some time. The delicate balance of secrets she was trying to weave behind the Sorceress's back was taking up a great deal of her attention.

"It's one of the glass creatures from the shelves," her daughter said, holding out her casting hand with fingers and palm flat, a red, shining shape resting in three pieces upon her palm.

"The phoenix toy from when I was little," her daughter clarified. "It fell from the shelf as I was passing to the library."

The phoenix's wings had broken—snapped from the mystical bird's spine. The Oracle's hand shook as she removed it from her daughter's open palm. She didn't dare look the girl in the eyes, afraid of what she would see staring back at her.

The gleaming ruby toy was cold in her hand.

Sweat prickled across the Oracle's brow. Two final messages from the beads, one for each wing. Two betrayals, waiting in the future.

The first would be the Sorceress, as she had antici-pated eventually occurring. One can only operate in the shadows for so long. But the second would be her daughter.

They would break the Oracle and likely the phoenix too.

The Oracle sighed. "Thank you for bringing this to me." She forced a smile and met her daughter's gaze. "Let me finish this correspondence, and I'll join you for the evening meal."

Her daughter bowed and slid out of the office and back into the family wing. Shutting off her study from her residence would draw suspicion which could be just as dangerous as taking no precaution at all.

The Oracle closed her hand around the broken glass bird. She winced as the glass pierced the skin of her palm. Blood that would bring the promise into being.

Years of watching for signs, anticipating the rebirth of Lilia, granddaughter of Verdigris, were finally coming to pass.

The broken bird might mean that the Sorceress and her daughter, in her future position as Oracle, would bring harm to the one reborn.

The Oracle would be dead and could do little but warn her allies of what the beads had shown her.

To fulfill her destiny, the returning soul would have to develop resilience. Like their world, she would need to be broken, but in that harm, she could help Eldura become what it was meant to be.

She completed her letters, rolled them into scrolls, and entrusted them to her messenger. Before joining her daughter, she tucked the broken pieces of the phoenix figurine into the spellbox atop her desk and placed a selenite wand on top of it to cleanse the figure's energy.

For untold years she'd been waiting to add the newest sign to the summoning box, the spell that recalled Lilia to return and save their world from impending destruction.

The Oracle smiled sadly to herself, remembering one of her mother's favorite mantras, fitting for their present crisis. *Upon the tangled threads of fate, we all have our part to play.*

CHAPTER THREE
KAILENA

The Oracle's letter reached her ally, Kailena, who met the owl-bearer on her daily walk through the forest outside the conclave of Willow Glen. Most in the conclave were reticent to leave the safety of the tree-line walkways interspersed far above the forest floor. Up there, they were safe from rogue maera and panthers but not so high up as to be in danger from the wyverns' nighttime hunts.

Kailena liked the noise of the understory, the chirruping of birds and chatter of red squirrels, the soft give of the earth beneath her feet.

Andeus would be waiting anxiously for her return, hovering outside the refractory and peering down the path for her, but he understood her need for time away from the conclave, even from him.

She needed to read the Oracle's missive in peace.

Kailena brushed long, garnet hair back over her shoulder and read:

I write to you of what I have seen and heard. By all accounts, Sanctuary will fall. With the city's demise, the Sorceress fears we will also lose the foundations of any hopes for joining the Cities on our own terms or remaining removed from them without show of force.

She believes that the remaining Cities, Respite above all, will wish to blame Lis-Maen for our insistence upon neutrality, what they hold to be a naïve dream and not the birthright of all. From her position within the Academia Magica, she rallies our mages to her cause with warnings that the Cities will punish our people for their own failures. They will use our ancestral lands as the buffer, the shield against the brunt of Alessandra's forces they have lacked for so long.

Kailena reread the first lines again, parsing through her friend's thoughts alongside the warning hidden beneath the message. The Sorceress's waning patience and desire to prove herself against the Cities' combined might was one of the hourglasses whose dwindling sieve meant they were running out of time.

You do not need to be a Seer, as I am, to understand what will next transpire. The Sorceress will never allow the Pentacle to be treated in this way. She would sacrifice the whole of Lis-Maen before surrendering a drop of power from the academy grounds in Delmoir. Her own movements against the Cities may provoke a response before the Cities have time to act of their own accord.

From those who have come before me, I have inherited the understanding that Alessandra has been planning for this through the ages. The betrayer goddess works within her own time. She remains independent of the fevered rush mortality inflicts upon mages and generals alike. She has no need to hurry, not while she believes she will soon gain control over the Wheel of Fate.

For now, the wheel rests safely beneath the soil of Lis-Maen. There it must stay, for the good of all.

A time of danger approaches. There is no alternative path around it. Strained alliances lead to misunderstanding and betrayal. We have but one spark of hope against the coming press of darkness—the phoenix, harbinger of Verdigris, draws near. As Lilith foresaw, the phoenix will return to us a wandering soul, that of Lilia, reembodied. She seeks the one to whom she bound herself, Hugh reincarnated. Without him, she has no hope of fulfilling her sacred destiny.

You know your role in this task—fate smiles upon your bloodline. May fortune favor you, my friend, and may Astralei grant our request.

Kailena rolled up the scroll and bowed her head, just as she would bow before the will of one poised above her in ranks.

Finally, after years of toil, reading the signs and seeking to prepare, the magical rebirth they'd been waiting for was near at hand.

She breathed deeply, savoring the dampness of the lower reaches of the forest. Andeus would be harder to convince. While Kailena's role placed her by necessity at the lead of their next task, the responsibility would fall to him to carry through.

ANDEUS

Kailena's eyes were bright as she strode toward Andeus.

The mere sight of her still set his blood aflame. "*Cora mi*," he sighed, opening his arms to embrace her. "Feeling cheerful this afternoon, are you, my love?"

A wide smile flashed across her face, obliterating the concern that had hung heavy upon her shoulders in recent days as the news from Sanctuary grew more and more dire.

"We've had a message."

"Oh?" He trailed his fingertips through the strands of her hair that had fallen out of her braid, savoring its softness. Maybe there was good news from the front for once.

"From the Oracle."

Andeus froze in place, his hand still poised at the back of her head. Kailena and the Oracle had become friends early in their relationship during one of the many negotiations and renegotiations between the Pentacle and the outlying conclaves. One of his oldest friends, a fae named Yvayne, had connected Kailena and the Oracle rather like she'd connected Andeus and Kailena in the first place.

In matters of the world, Yvayne and the Oracle were often of one accord, and he knew how much Kailena valued their esteem.

He only wished he could trust the three of them to be more cautious of themselves and their futures. That he could trust Yvayne and the Oracle to have his partner's best interests at heart rather than their own.

"What did she write to you?"

Kailena drew back from him and her gaze danced along the suspended bridges that hung between the trees. The conclave of Willow Glen was special in that regard—it was one of few settlements that had been able to maintain its original treetop structure, in part due to his and Kailena's innovations with the elements.

"It's coded. I'm sure she's worried about surveillance."

Andeus nodded. This was not news to him, but it didn't answer his question either.

His partner wetted her lips, the sense of anticipation he'd detected ebbing as she tried to gauge his emotions. "She received a sign, definitively, that it's time for Lilia to be reborn. Exactly as Yvayne has been telling us."

He sighed a laugh—how was one to react to such news? "Just like that?"

Immediately, Kailena's mood shifted. "How else would you propose we go about it?"

Andeus crossed his arms over his chest and leaned back against one of the support poles in the interior of the refractory. They'd built the ailing hut up together. The orbs of light they'd designed flickered overhead, pricks of light trapped in clouds of swirling darkness, waiting to be pulled into the canopy to renew their energy in the sun.

"You cannot ask me to be cavalier about a magical summoning ritual to call back a soul from Astralei, one that bears such an inherent and palpable danger to you. Yes, the Oracle faces the threat of the Sorceress. Yes, Yvayne faces—" Andeus waved his hand through the air.

The only being he could imagine having a longer list of enemies than Yvayne was Alessandra herself. "Untold conflicts," he finally said, shaking his head.

"I thought you believed in this." The softness of her voice was a dagger in his side.

Andeus dropped his voice as well. "Of course I do." He wanted to open his arms to her, to reassure her in his embrace. "But you know as well as I do—better even— what such magic requires. It is not without cost."

He swallowed the conflicting emotions that threatened to strangle him at the weight of what they were attempting. Andeus knew better than to believe Kailena could be dissuaded. Had he thought the trial before them would be easier with time?

They were not the first to try to summon Lilia, believing that without her intervention, their world would meet its end. If previous summonings had been successful, they had not lasted long enough for Yvayne to sense the return of Lilia's spirit. As a fellow granddaughter of the vanished titan of nature, Verdigris, Yvayne was convinced that she would have known of Lilia's rebirth.

The accounts she'd uncovered in her work alongside the Order of Verdigris—the secret organization that he'd been born into, where he'd met Kailena and fallen for her fiery spirit almost immediately, though she took quite a bit longer to fall for his quieter, less bold temperament—were unequivocal on the point of the cost for the ritual. Whether Lilia desired to return or not was immaterial. For the mortals demanding such a boon, there was an equal cost in blood.

Kailena paled but gave no other sign of the fear that was more than natural—that was innate. The actions they were discussing went against the instincts instilled since birth, the will to survive. "It is no more than those who came before us did."

Andeus shook his head. "That doesn't mean we have to follow in their footsteps." His voice warbled with the fear that Kailena refused to show.

His partner took his hand, her knuckles whitening as she squeezed it in hers. "They entrusted their legacy to us. Your parents. The agents of the Sapphire Circle. The lorekeepers who secreted the ritual out of the ruins of Alessandra's holdings in Scourge. The daimon who survived the extermination brought on by the empress of Verrain. They gave their lives in hopes that such a day might come."

Andeus met Kailena's gaze. He'd learned very early in their relationship that there was no use arguing with her once her mind was set. If Verdigris or Lilith appeared before her, they might be able to change her mind. But for a mortal such as himself whose only claim to deep wisdom was the love he bore for her, such a feat was not possible.

When Kailena's mind focused upon a task she believed in, there was no hope of swaying her from it.

"May I see the missive?"

She nodded, keeping her lips pressed together. "The Oracle sent word to Yvayne as well."

The tiny spark of hope that had lingered in his chest faltered. With the fae's assent, any hope of resistance would be one-sided. He could not outweigh the three of them.

As a young elf, he hadn't given much thought to the rearing of a child. In his and Kailena's earliest discussions, he had believed that they were merely speaking in hypotheticals, almost like one would try on alternate endings of folklore only to conclude that, however tragic, the stories were the way they were for a reason.

If he had known what he would be asked to bear—deliberately engaging in magic that would likely bring about the death of his partner, elevating himself to the status of someone capable of raising a reborn heroine, a granddaughter of Verdigris, a returned soul in a new form—would he have walked away?

The answer came to him slowly as he read over the letter from the Oracle, only occasionally consulting the code she and Kailena had devised for their communications. He'd been raised to await Lilia's return, she who would bring them one step closer to the return of Verdigris who would remake the world as it was intended to be.

The part of him that valued his partner above all else raged at the very thought of what he was considering. But an even older flame, one conceived in his mother's stories, during the lessons he learned at his father's knee, rejoiced that he might live to see such an age emerge. That he might look into the green eyes of the one returned and help her become who she was meant to be.

He sighed heavily as he completed the missive. "On the full moon, then?" The night marked a significant convergence the astrologers had been waiting for—the birth-cycle, a nine month period, that would end with a rare celestial sight—twin dark moons. If their conception was successful, that would be the sign under which their child would be born.

Kailena sat stiffly beside him. She inclined her head. "So may it be."

"So let it be done."

With their vow to one another made, there was little left to do beyond seeing it through. Andeus held up his end of their arrangement and resisted questioning the choice they had made, together.

Or the choice Kailena had made that, out of love for her, he felt compelled to support.

The days passed and the moon waxed, her growing face a celestial hourglass marking short the days until Andeus's life forever changed.

On the night of the full greater moon, the constellation of Lilith shone down upon him and Kailena, her position in the sky marking the end of winter.

Of greater significance was the constellation's signaling of an even more profound chance—the rebirth of one long absent from the world. This returning soul would have the ability to reunite the six elemental powers and restore their world. The Hexblade, Lilith's agents had come to call her. The Harbinger of Verdigris. Lilia reborn.

CHAPTER FOUR

YVAYNE

THE EMERAUDE

Much has changed since the Fall of the First Age, Yvayne wrote in her private journal.

But in this, all is as it ever was. We recall Lilia through our promise to Verdigris, through the tireless work of Lilith and her agents through the ages. We ask that she return to us the spark of her grandmother. Hers and mine.

Yvayne lowered her eagle-feather quill and sat back from the desk she kept within the dragon's library, hidden deep within the Emeraude. She was the last remaining granddaughter of Verdigris who still drew breath. Even those like her and her cousins, Lilith—the daughter of a goddess and a titan—had passed on.

The fae ran her tongue over her teeth. Was it possible for another to understand the loneliness of there being no other beings like oneself? She smiled, shaking her head. If they succeeded in recalling Lilia and forging her into the Hexblade, the recurring soul might understand.

The druids were the closest reflection to the union of the six elements, as it had been before the Fall of the First Age, before Verdigris divided herself into three—the first of a great many sacrifices in the face of war and bloodshed.

Yvayne reached for her quill but drew her hand back. Wasn't she about to do precisely what she had condemned others for doing before her? Proceeding with recalling Lilia's soul would put a death sentence over Kailena, cruel in its own way, and even more difficult to ask Andeus to bear. Was this truly the next step on the path forward? Or was she taking the simplest and most obvious way, forging a path in sacrifice and blood?

In centuries past, she had consulted Arcanum scholars, those who worked at the Academia Magica, those who performed their research in the great city of Beacon, and the priestesses who served the Grand Matrons of the Emeraude. They called the old magic Yvayne and her allies were trying to breathe back into the world a phoenix soul—a name forged in part by promises Hugh and Lilia were said to have made to one another, that they would find each other through the ages.

Whether they called her the Hexblade, as the agents of Lilith and the Pentacle did, or the phoenix, it was the responsibility of one with such a long memory as Yvayne possessed to ask—in the Hexblade's wake, how many more would perish? She would not be a bringer of peace, this new Lilia. She could not be. Their world was too divided. Alessandra had seen to that.

If the Sorceress learned of her, she would see the Hexblade lead Lis-Maen into the war. The Cities would stop at nothing to claim the reborn Lilia's power for their own.

Yvayne sighed to herself. The answer before them was clear.

The Hexblade would have to be forged in secret, protected until she came of age.

She and the Oracle would do all they could to shield the child as she grew, but some of that protection would appear as neglect—above all, they could not draw the eye of those who would use the Hexblade for their own ends to the girl before she was ready.

And are you so different, my child?

Yvayne froze as the internalized voice of her mother whistled through her mind.

Are you not using this child for your own ends?

As though you have any right to speak on such a subject, Yvayne shot back before she could stop herself. She pressed her fingertips to her temples. This might be the first phase of madness, arguing with oneself.

It was in following her mother's example that she knew how useful the soul of a child might be. The pressure of one so small carrying the hopes and dreams of an entire people. Especially when she was sent off on her own.

Yvayne clenched her jaw and forcibly plucked the feather quill from its holder. She dipped it into the ink and flattened the parchment before her. The Oracle would heed her instructions. She knew what was at stake.

I have given a great deal of thought to your concerns,

Yvayne wrote to the Oracle. *Do not think I relay the following lightly.*

The child must be protected as she grows so that her power can come fully into its own. You know how great a weapon one blessed as the Hexblade is sure to be would become in the wrong hands.

Our best path is to secret her away in the forest, hide her among the druids. Andeus will protect her.

To keep ambitious eyes from the child, we will need you to create a binding accord on behalf of the foresters—whatever you have to do to secure the arrangement, see to it that the Sorceress cannot pull her offerings from the ranks of the outskirts conclaves. This will ensure the survival of Kailena and Andeus's child into adulthood and give her magic a chance to take root.

Unfortunately for the Sorceress's own plans, her ambition in this case played right into Yvayne and the lorekeepers' hands. She would be so focused on bringing the united elemental powers into being that she wouldn't question the seemingly small obstacle of a few foresters' settlements seeking a reprieve from her experiments for a decade or two.

The step she had prescribed to the Oracle provided their efforts with a contingency while also exacting a blood cost. If they were wrong about who the child had been born to, the baby born beneath the twin dark moons, the sign seen once or twice in a century, the measures they were preparing to take would provide a protective buffer for that child as well.

When her mother had expelled Yvayne from the Shadowlands to preserve the memory of their people, she had learned about the blood required for the old magic of the world. Protecting the foresters' children born under the twin dark moons would make those born elsewhere in Lis-Maen more vulnerable to the Sorceress and her search for "offerings."

They had not opted into such a sacrifice, but it was the role of those like Yvayne to demand it of them, even if she wished a different outcome were possible.

The other children would be the first to fall to make way for the Hexblade. None of the competing forces warring for control over Eldura would blink at the cost of a few hundred lives, especially those of the elves and mages of Lis-Maen.

So however much it grieved her to think of them, Yvayne grit her teeth and turned her gaze from their fate. They were not the first sacrifices to be made, nor would they be the last.

CHAPTER FIVE
THE ORACLE

The sharp rap of a knock pulled the Oracle's attention from Yvayne's newest letter. She had already begun drafting an agreement to send to Andeus and many of the other conclave elders across the forest settlements encouraging them to set particular terms against "centralization and aggression" on behalf of the Pentacle.

"Come in," she called. It was unlike her guards to disrupt her while she was working, but if one of the apprentices had need of her help, she liked to be open to their queries.

Her eyes widened as the Sorceress strode into her office—in nearly all instances across their decades of working together, the Sorceress had bidden the Oracle to come to her rooms, not the other way around.

"The alchemists and their families have arrived," the Sorceress said evenly, glancing about the Oracle's study. Her dark eyes glittered with the promise such an occurrence entailed.

Those unfortunate enough to have fallen prey to the Sorceress's trackers would not find her a kind taskmaster. She would demand they pay for what was taken from Lis-Maen—the distilled power of the elements the Cities used to harness their alchemical weapons.

The Sorceress believed that the Cities had stolen the elements in their raw form from Lis-Maen within the last century, though none of the other sects of the Pentacle could corroborate such a claim. The Cities said the elements came directly from the champions appointed by the elemental titans but, as they refused to explain *how* such a transference occurred, the Sorceress held to her beliefs and the plans of reprisal they inspired.

She tried to hide her surprise at the Sorceress's sudden visit. "Would you like me to accompany you?"

The Sorceress smirked. "I thought you might enjoy the exercise. A reminder of what's at stake, for all of us."

Chills ran down the Oracle's lower back. She dropped the missive from Yvayne onto her desk, conscious of what the letter might mean in the wrong hands. So casual a movement might be enough to convince the Sorceress that there was nothing secretive or untoward in the Oracle's shock at her appearance.

She pushed her chair back and rose from the desk, plucking a shawl from a hook along the wall as she crossed the room to the Sorceress's side.

Leaving the letter behind went against her better instincts, but inviting the Sorceress's suspicion was the more dangerous of the two options. Besides, her daughter was the only one in her wing with access to her rooms. It wasn't as though one of the Sorceress's spies could infiltrate her private quarters.

"Are these alchemists from Respite?" the Oracle asked, hoping to draw her own mind from the fae's letter and the partially composed replies she'd drafted for Andeus and the other conclave leaders.

"Most of them, from what I've gathered. Their airship . . . crashed in the bay while blown off course on a transport to Sanctuary." The Sorceress grinned. "Hopefully the Army of Light didn't need the backup supply of alchemists' fire."

"Fire alchemists?" The Oracle paused mid stride to take in the ramifications of the boon to their efforts. Alchemists' fire was remarkably powerful, more so than any of the other distilled elements and, for its volatility, incredibly difficult to craft without mortal peril. She recovered herself and resumed her quick strides beside her fellow Face.

When the Sorceress first began her own experiments in alchemists' fire, the Oracle had lent her several of her own apprentices whose Sight was underdeveloped to aid in the approximation of the substance. One had returned without eyebrows as they'd been singed off. The other had not returned at all.

"Fortunately for us, they had a few generalists among their number," the Sorceress added. "Not exactly what we need for our future plans but enough to suffice for the present and allow our experiments to move forward."

They crossed the sunny lawn of the academy grounds and passed through one of the carefully tended groves. As they wound their way toward a side entrance within the Sorceress's tower that led directly to the dungeons, the Sorceress expounded upon the steps of her grand plan for creating the "Hexblade" warriors.

With the generalist alchemists, she explained, they could distill the base components of each element into an injectable form. Between the liquefied elements and the use of ancient runes and binding spells, all that would remain would be to find enough candidates who could withstand the raw power of the elements.

"I know the Cities would object to us standing in for the titans and the titans' will in selecting their own champions," the Sorceress continued, "but I find such a position to be myopic at best and, more promising still, a dangerous underestimation of our might."

The Oracle's lips thinned at the Sorceress's determination to provoke the Cities. Stealing their alchemists from their military transports was daring enough, but should news of the Hexblade plot reach the wrong ears within the Cities' ranks, it could mean open war.

Perhaps that was the Sorceress's ultimate goal. For herself, such a path seemed a greater risk than Lis-Maen was prepared to weather.

"You are quiet," the Sorceress observed. "You do not approve of my plan?"

"Apologies, Sorceress," the Oracle added quickly. She snatched at the stray strands of her thoughts that longed to return to the letter on her desk. There had to be a loophole Andeus could use to protect the child he and Kailena would conceive, something he might share with the other foresters whose children would be born around the same time. She shook her head, pushing the threads of her scheme away until she could pursue them in solitude. "I was only trying to anticipate what the Cities' response to such a move on our part might be. The more extreme among their number would perceive the Hexblade project as blasphemy."

"And you think that means we should limit our own magical research?" The sharp warning in the Sorceress's tone snapped against the Oracle's already fraying nerves.

"Far from it." She forced a smile and met the dark gaze of her companion. "I am only trying to work through the particulars, make sure I understand the stakes before we meet with the alchemists."

"They will not disappoint, I assure you."

Two guards covered in weapons waited outside the hidden side entrance to the dungeons beneath the Sorceress's towers. They bowed at her approach and opened the door.

After the Oracle passed through on the Sorceress's heels, the guards secured the door shut behind them. The echo of the solid wood thrummed outward along the dark stone hallway that wound beneath the tower grounds. The Oracle blinked rapidly, waiting for her eyes to adjust to the dim light. She wasn't sure whether she imagined soft cries and muffled sniffling or if the Sorceress's captives lingered nearby.

The Sorceress led her deeper beneath the tower. Dark corridors branched off the main passageway, each containing a line of closed doors. Muffled screams echoed from a couple of the hallways. Most were more frightening for their silence.

On occasion, they passed one of the Sorceress's masked guards who bowed to their mistress as she passed.

The unspoken meaning was clear—no one would find their way out of the cavern prison without the Sorceress's knowledge and permission.

"They're waiting for us just ahead," the Sorceress said, indicating a turn in their path onto a more brightly lit hallway.

Unlike the initial passageways which were only intermittently illuminated by flickering firestone sconces embedded within the walls, the new hallways the Sorceress led her onto were much brighter, with flickering water orbs and selenite lanterns interspersed between the sconces that lent a flickering, hauntingly pleasant light to the surroundings. It reminded the Oracle of her own study, where each light source was surrounded by opal quartz stones, which granted a warmth to her space but, somehow, the effect was colder here. Almost as though they were drowning, but underground instead of underwater.

Any sense of familiarity fell away as the ever-present guards at the end of this second hall opened creaking iron doors onto a wide prison area. Cells of varying sizes held huddled alchemists. Some bore the bruises and singed hair and clothing of their airship crash while others who sat stiffly with heads lowered bore the tell-tale signs of torture.

Her stomach twisted as she spied children in their midst, remembering the Sorceress's stated plan to acquire the alchemists' family members so they might be made more pliable toward her own ends.

Only one group glared back in open defiance, hatred glittering behind their eyes as they stared down her and the Sorceress. The Oracle suspected they were the ones who had yet to give up the locations of their families after seeing what befell those who caved.

"We have begun work based on the first drips of information they've been willing to share and that we've taken the time to corroborate," the Sorceress said, gesturing to the wall on the far side of the cells where several burbling concoctions sat over small fires, each surrounded by a complex array of pipes.

A few of the Sorceress's apprentices hovered nearby with worn notebooks in hand, scribbling notes onto parchment pages.

"You're corroborating their information so they don't take drastic measures to preserve the Cities' secrets?"

"More or less."

Before she could ask for further clarification, a familiar shape waltzed out of the shadowy corner of the room toward the two women. The Oracle's daughter approached, her robe whispering over the stone behind her.

The Oracle frowned. "What are you doing here?" An uneasy prickling sensation spread from the back of her neck down to the curve of her spine. The beads had warned her about two betrayals—was this the beginning of the first, or was that already underway?

"Your daughter has kindly agreed to assist me in seeing our guests . . . taken care of."

It was difficult to read either her daughter or the Sorceress's expressions in the flickering light from the glowing firestones embedded in the walls.

The Oracle wanted to pull her daughter aside, to scold her for such an association, for torturing mages in the shadows for no greater crime than their place of birth and the alliance that had naturally occurred because of it, but there would be no surer way of showing her hand to the Sorceress, and Kailena and Andeus needed more time. Yvayne as well.

The unease in her gut tightened as she perceived the depths of deceit that would be asked of her when she stood before the alchemists and their families. The show she would have to make over the coming weeks.

Yvayne had been right about the blood cost of what they were attempting. How had she not anticipated such an outcome?

"Where would you like me to begin my efforts?" the Oracle asked the Sorceress, affecting as disinterested a tone as possible.

"You needn't worry yourself with starting work this early in the process," the Sorceress mused. "For today, I thought you might like to see how well your daughter and I work together, and then we'll find a place for you in future sessions."

Even those among the captive alchemists who had held jaws and fists tightly blanched at the Sorceress's words. They understood the meaning hidden beneath. *They were to be part of a show.*

The Oracle inhaled slowly, drawing in her own feeling of powerlessness before the events unspooling beyond her. Would their end goal be worth the sacrifices made in this room? Was this what it would take to secure the future of their world?

This and more, her inner voice answered. The Oracle shivered. She knew it was true.

"I'll be over here so as to remain out of your way," she said, hand tightening around her shawl.

In the hours that followed, she wasn't sure what was worse—the alchemists screaming under torment until they grew hoarse, the stillness of the bodies of those who could take no more, or the gleam in her daughter's eyes as she discovered the power that a mage untethered could wield.

The Oracle held her peace until she made it back to her private rooms where she retched in her bathing chamber. She spent a few hours soaking in lukewarm water, asking the ancients to show her something else, to grant her additional reassurance that she was walking the right path, that she wasn't identical to those she and Yvayne thought of as enemies.

No such reassurance came.

Her fingers wrinkled from the water and with a persistent shiver running down her spine, the Oracle wrapped herself in her thickest robe and returned to her desk. It was precisely as she'd left it.

She composed her missive to Andeus and the other conclave leaders across the forests of Lis-Maen with precise instructions for the collective bargain they were to strike.

The Oracle tied each of the missives to one of her

trusted parliament of owls and sent them off into the forest wilds in the dead of night.

The alchemists who had perished that evening would not have done so in vain, she promised herself.

There would be a blood cost in payment for what the Sorceress had taken from them. And it would begin beneath the twin dark moons when a phoenix soul returned to their world once more. One with the power to remake Eldura anew.

CHAPTER SIX
THE ORACLE

The Oracle smiled to herself as she perused the packed shelves of her sect's library. It was here that the wisdom of generations, gathered over thousands of years had been relocated from the outskirts of Lis-Maen to this tower upon the grounds of the Academia Magica so her line and that of the other Faces might work as one to ensure the future of Lis-Maen and the various expressions of natural magic within their world.

Each of the great civilizations of Eldura claimed to possess the grandest library. The Oracle shook her head as she traced the gilded leather spines of past Oracles' journals. Such competitiveness missed the point, she believed. Whether it was located within the depths of the Emeraude, the great halls of Bastion, the temples of Beacon, the garrisons of Respite, the ancient trees of the Sapphire Circle, or the private libraries cultivated and maintained by the Faces of the Pentacle, each collection spoke to the unique values of their respective cultures. The value of the collection was relative, was it not?

The scholars of Bastion could no more use the records contained within her hall than she could make use of the careful transcriptions of Ilona's priests in Beacon.

She had promised Andeus that she would search her archives for any record of past attempts at recalling a departed soul that didn't result in the death of the one bringing the new soul into being. His letters were growing more anxious with each passing moon as his transition into fatherhood grew nearer.

Since her daughter's conception, she had known that she and she alone would guide her. There was no counterpart to the Oracle, only the Oracle herself. But that had not been Andeus's dream for his family.

Perhaps Yvayne had been right and they were asking too much of him, but the Oracle wasn't willing to give up on the possibility that Kailena's life might be spared, if only they were willing to work hard enough to bring such a possibility about. If she could keep Andeus from despair and keep Yvayne from an over reliance upon the magical practicalities of sacrifice, they might find a way.

"Ma'am?" A panicked voice rang out from the main aisle of the Oracle's library. One of her new guards.

He called again, louder this time.

The Oracle dropped the tome she'd selected back onto its shelf and rushed to the end of the aisle, holding the hem of her robes as she ran.

The guard's eyes were wide when they met hers. One

of her spies hovered just behind the guard's shoulder, a woman she'd secreted into the Sorceress's household after Kailena's news of conception had reached her.

"What is it?" The Oracle glanced between them, fear clutching her throat.

"Your daughter, ma'am," the guard began.

Titans forbid—

"The Sorceress has taken her captive," the spy added.

The pleasant silence of the library hall fell away, replaced by a roaring in the Oracle's ears. "Where?" she demanded. She hurried toward the library exit before the guard and spy could answer—this, at least, she already knew.

"She's in the dungeons beneath the Sorceress's tower, ma'am," the spy said, confirming the Oracle's suspicions. Foolish, to not have foreseen such a development. The Sorceress had added experiments she called "offerings" to the remaining alchemists beneath her tower.

The offerings were the second stage of the Sorceress's Hexblade plan—with the distilled elements in hand, it was time to discover how they might be wielded.

The only true mystery before her was why the Sorceress had captured her daughter. Had she discovered Yvayne's missives? Unearthed their alternate Hexblade scheme? Or was it something else entirely, some twist of the Sorceress's unending ambition?

"Gather reinforcements and meet me outside the dungeons," the Oracle ordered her guard. There remained every possibility that they'd have to fight their way through the Sorceress's defenses, cutting deeply into the heavily guarded dungeon halls the Oracle had first entered several months before.

Had the Sorceress been plotting this move against her even then? Showing the Oracle how outmatched she would be if matters soured between them?

Her thoughts jumbled as she tried again to tease out what had invited the Sorceress's animosity—why strike against her now? Had one of her own agents betrayed her? Had the Sorceress seen through the coordinated diplomatic efforts of the forest conclaves to shield Andeus and Kailena's child and was punishing the Oracle's daughter for her mother's schemes?

"Alert the others. Maintain your cover if you can," she ordered the spy.

She could replace those sworn to her and placed within the Sorceress's service if need be, though she couldn't make the mistake of operating along too short a timeframe in her own plans. Though the Sorceress was without the gift of Sight, she was always playing to win the long game.

The Oracle would have to match her. The Sorceress had gone too far this time. Even if her spy was mistaken about the implications of whatever had transpired, she should have put a stop to her daughter's association with the Sorceress when she'd first found her in the dungeons with the alchemists.

The Hexblade plan was too dark—it twisted any who came near.

A small army of reinforcements fell into line behind the Oracle as she charged across the academy grounds.

The captain of her guard shouted orders, sending

some to scout ahead, others to form a cordon around the Oracle to protect her from magical attack or ambush.

They knew better than to slow her down or get in her way.

Across the academy grounds, cohorts of students and clusters of apprentices rushed away from the Oracle and her guards. The scant few who were brave enough to attempt to interfere were quickly shooed away and sent back to their dormitories for safety.

The tang of blood was sharp on the air. It wouldn't be long until it ran free—either hers or the Sorceress's.

Three armed guards sprinted up the side stairwell, pikes clutched against their chests.

The Oracle waved her hand, casting a ripple in the threads of fate that sent them flying to the side, thumping against the trunk of a tree one after the next before falling into a heap of tangled limbs.

One of her guards protested when he saw that she meant to descend the stairs first.

The words died in his throat with a single glare.

Her rage only faltered slightly at the bottom of the stair where the Sorceress's elite guards waited—only two, as had been the case upon her first arrival. "Madam Oracle," one said with a bow, "we have been expecting you."

"I should think so. My daughter is being held captive inside."

The guard simply inclined his head. "The Sorceress has granted you leave to pass, but you must enter alone."

Her own personal guard wouldn't hear of such a plan. "Absolutely out of the—"

"Silence," the Oracle corrected him. She hadn't seen her spies in the Sorceress's service on the grounds and could only assume they'd been able to regain their positions. She would not be truly alone inside.

"To be more specific as to the terms," the guard continued, "our lady says it depends upon how much blood you would like to pool upon your hands." His tone remained even as he spoke, the threat written plain upon the bulging muscles of his arms and shoulders.

The guard turned to the Oracle's captain. "My lady likewise promises that the Oracle will emerge shortly." He bowed his head. "I understand the code you are under as it binds me as well."

The two men watched one another warily for another moment before returning their attention to the Oracle. At her word, they would fight to the death while she shoved past and made her way into the tunnels beneath the Sorceress's tower.

Unlike her rival, the Oracle did not believe those of a lesser magical gifting to be expendable—they each had a fate written upon the beads, each had their part to play in the larger plans unspooling across their world.

The Oracle turned to her guard. "You have served me faithfully and with honor. Wait here until I return."

His jaw tensed, but the guard said nothing further as he inclined his head, submitting himself to her will.

"Has your lady offered an escort?" she asked the guard, glancing at his fellow.

The guard who had been speaking bowed to her as well. "Most certainly." He rapped against the door with his knuckles, and the heavy metal grate swung open, revealing a small troupe of guards waiting inside.

Her retinue stiffened behind her, but they did not falter from her ruling. She had trained them well to trust her Sight over what they could perceive with their own senses.

"Take me to my daughter," she ordered the leader of the cluster of guards.

The elf she'd addressed had bright gold eyes and dark hair worn in braids woven tightly against her scalp. Golden tattoos wove along her bare arms, the skin around them red and swollen. Beads of sweat clustered along her brow.

The Oracle's eyes widened, but she said nothing about the guard's condition. The Sorceress had already begun her elemental tests and had spread her experiments beyond the ranks of the offerings she had selected.

This guard had been injected with the distilled element of light. The Oracle didn't believe the guard would outlive the infection the element seemed to have provoked.

The elf gestured for the Oracle to proceed to the front of the column.

The Oracle kept her head high as she walked. With eight guards clustered around her and others lurking in the shadows, it would be difficult for her to make her escape, even more challenging the further in they walked. She resisted the urge to glance back at her own retinue before the reinforced door slammed shut behind them, deepening the shadows of the Sorceress's dungeons.

Distant drippings from still-living stone punctuated the stomping footsteps of the Oracle's escort. The same sniffling echoed out of corners like her first foray into the dungeons. The scents of unspent magic and decay layered unpleasantly one over the next, sparks and rot mingling, each worsening the other.

With each hurried stride, the Oracle left behind what she might have done differently, the additional precautions she could have taken.

As they neared the laboratory chambers, they passed clusters of the kidnapped alchemists and their families. A woman with dark eyes glared at the Oracle from the depths of her prison cell, her pale children holding one another and pressed against her side while on her lap, a man with a high fever cradled the stump of his arm against his body. The man turned his face away from the procession.

She understood the glare, whether or not it was deserved. If she and Yvayne were willing to lose a dear friend to recall Lilia—in the service of saving millions from Alessandra's purges—she wouldn't hesitate to lose a stranger as well.

But that was not the same as losing her daughter.

The Oracle's breath caught in her chest as the muted sounds of the Sorceress's voice called her forward. She picked up her pace, the guards around her following suit.

Around the next bend, the Sorceress's words became clear though the laboratory door remained shut. "Tell me of your mother's treachery," the Sorceress demanded, her voice cold and unfeeling.

A sizzle of flesh and her daughter's sharp scream were all that answered the demand.

Without thought for her retinue of guards, the Oracle sprinted ahead and shoved through the final dungeon door.

She stopped short, mouth ajar, as she found her daughter trapped beneath a harsh beam of light, restrained against a slanted table, a brand hot upon her arm and blood dripping from her opposite side onto the floor.

"Enough," the Oracle pronounced, not taking her eyes from her child.

The Sorceress slid forward into the slat of light from overhead, the cold white beam illuminating a cruel smile before casting the hollows of her face in shadow—a grinning skull. "Only when I say so," the Sorceress answered, barely suppressing her glee.

The Oracle tightened her hands into fists, ignoring the presence of the guards filing in behind her, the solid shutting and barring of the door, or the dozen mages waiting inside with a pair of tormentors. "No," the Oracle shot back. "This is too far. You are without offspring and do not understand."

"Mama, please," her daughter begged, tears bright in her eyes. "You have to tell her what she needs to know or—"

"Quiet, you," the second tormentor seethed, striding forward with a blade in hand.

Without thinking, the Oracle flicked her wrist, baring her palm to the second torturer. Bright purple vines sprang into being and wrapped around the torturer. He screamed and writhed as the pustules of fate along the underside of the vines burned through his clothing. The burning of flesh was painful—the Oracle couldn't help a cruel smile of her own as the one who'd injured her daughter screamed in terror—but the revisited memories twisted from the worst moments of someone's life were far worse to endure. Even if the torturer lived through the recovery from her magic's burns, he would never escape the memories she had reawakened and twisted into monstrous form within his mind.

The Sorceress clicked her tongue behind her teeth. "Now, now, Oracle, this is hardly the time for such rash action, especially given the vulnerable position you and your daughter find yourselves in."

Keeping her gaze on the Oracle, the Sorceress gestured to her first torturer, the one who had just applied a sizzling brand to her daughter's skin—the stench of charred flesh was still sharp in the room.

As one, the Oracle's escort strode forward and grasped her wrists, two others at her shoulders.

A stone sank in the Oracle's gut as the Sorceress continued to watch her. She had acted rashly, and now her daughter would pay the price.

The torturer waited for the Sorceress's signal before he laid aside the brand and took up the discarded knife from the man still writhing on the ground.

"A punishment for grossly underestimating the situation you are in," the Sorceress said with a nod to the torturer.

Her daughter screamed as the man slashed a dagger across her cheek with a spray of crimson.

The Oracle gasped as though she'd been struck. "Please," she begged the Sorceress. "Let her go. She doesn't know anything."

The Sorceress froze—head back, eyes glittering. "I cannot believe your daughter matters so little to you." She didn't even bother to look at the torture she was overseeing, that she was forcing the Oracle to witness.

What they were asking Kailena to do was cruel enough. Could Yvayne truly expect her to lose her own child in Lilia's name? Was this the blood sacrifice demanded for a returned soul? She had hoped that part of their research had been mistaken and had never imagined it to be so far-reaching.

"Mama, help!" her daughter cried. Tears fell freely down her daughter's cheeks, each one a sharp blade stabbing into the Oracle's abdomen.

"Last chance," the Sorceress snapped.

The torturer she'd attacked lay twitching on the dungeon floor, breathing heavily. With a twitch of her eye, she could renew the man's torment, but the cost to her daughter was too great.

"Alright," the Oracle conceded, returning her gaze to her daughter. "I'll tell you."

She had hoped to see relief glimmer back at her—did her daughter know what her vulnerability to the Sorceress might cost them all? Not just those who lived upon Eldura, but the generations to come—

Instead, an unreadable expression flashed across her daughter's face, something akin to spite.

The Oracle shook away her observation. Nothing

more than the faulty light of the dungeons and a heightened situation.

"Tie her up," the Sorceress ordered.

"Let my daughter go," the Oracle answered, struggling against the tightened hold of the Sorceress's guards.

"Once I have what I need."

"Your implements will not be necessary," the Oracle said, glaring at the lone remaining torturer. She straightened against the table they'd tied her to, summoning as much regal energy as she could muster under the circumstances.

With only a few moments to calculate the fallout of her choices, the Oracle decided to commit one betrayal in order to disguise the other. Surely Yvayne would understand. She was the most powerful of the four of them by far, certainly more so than an expectant Kailena with a worried Andeus to defend her.

The Oracle told the Sorceress of her and Yvayne's plot to bring about a Hexblade of their own, one who would remain independent of the Pentacle should the need for such a mage arise. "I was jealous of your power," she lied, "fearful of the imbalance it might give rise to in Lis-Maen."

The Sorceress's gaze narrowed. "I don't believe you." She flicked her wrist much as the Oracle had done before.

The Oracle's world gave way to pain.

"That's enough!" her daughter's insistent plea was the first sound beyond her own screams and the thrashing of her body that brought the Oracle out of the Sorceress's spell.

Her rival's eyes flashed. "There will be more if your mother continues to hide the truth. You and Yvayne feared something else. Tell me."

The Oracle's thoughts were fragmented. Already the lies she'd woven to protect Andeus and Kailena were unraveling. She could not tell the Sorceress of their child. She would swallow her own tongue first—though the Sorceress had ways of preventing even that from occurring.

"It's a prophecy, surrounding the Hexblade. I feared for the distant conclaves," the Oracle added. "They are essential to Lis-Maen's future and the revival of wild magic. That is what the Hexblade might do. I feared such a being falling fully under your power."

At this the Sorceress's smile returned. "I should have known Ravenna's rejected daughter wouldn't be able to resist so great a temptation. Yvayne's role has been so much less, hmm, *impactful* than that of the other grand-daughters of Verdigris."

The Oracle's heart leaped in her chest, her pulse surging along her limbs at the mention of the grand-daughters. Whatever the cost, she could not give up Lilia's return, not with so much death already lurching toward them.

"This is the motivation behind the outer conclaves' resistance to the offerings, is it?" Strangely, the Sorceress turned toward the Oracle's daughter. "We could allow such a notion to continue, allow Yvayne to fall into our trap while the conclaves believe themselves and their offspring to be safe. There are plenty of others to serve in the trials. How long did you give them?" The

Sorceress turned back to the Oracle. "Close to twenty years?"

The Oracle's lips parted but she could not speak. The expression her daughter had made was beginning to fit into place. But it could not be.

"I think she's worked it out," her daughter said, the first prickles of a smile twisting at the corner of her mouth.

The Sorceress's full grin returned. "Is that so?"

She flicked her wrist toward the Oracle's daughter once more.

"No!" the Oracle cried, unable to help herself.

A peal of laughter burst from the Sorceress's lips as the chains fell away from her daughter, freeing her and falling to the dungeon floor. "Even so near to the end, she has not puzzled it together. And for one blessed with Sight?" The Sorceress's shrieks of delight jarred the Oracle's already frayed nerves.

"It is too much, too much," she said, dabbing at the corners of her eyes.

The Oracle's daughter was brushing off her clothing. She crossed to one of the side tables and began donning the jewelry she'd discarded, each bracelet jangling softly against the growing stack upon her wrist.

"We'll need to look back through their missives," the Sorceress said, her attention still on the Oracle's daughter. "See if there are any additional wrinkles in her alliance with Yvayne. I learned years ago not to underestimate the fae, however uninteresting she at first appears."

The Oracle's mouth hung ajar, watching her

daughter put herself back together and prepare to abandon her within this chamber. The chamber she'd entered in order to save her child, abandoning the plot that would save the rest of Eldura.

So foolish, so foolish, a voice sang over and over in her mind.

The beads had warned her, as had the glass phoenix.

She'd burned all the letters from Kailena, hadn't she? But what if one arrived before Kailena and Andeus learned of her fate? What if Yvayne was too busy in the Emeraude to notice the shift in magic of the Pentacle—

"Aren't you forgetting something?" the Sorceress glowered down at the Oracle's treacherous daughter.

Halfway to the door, her daughter froze and turned back. "What do you mean?"

"You wish to take on your mother's mantle, do you not?"

"Y-yes." Her daughter cleared her throat. "It is my inheritance."

"Precisely," the Sorceress answered. "The whole of Lis-Maen knows of the secret ritual that transfers the Sight from mother to daughter among the Oracle line."

The tears that had wet the Oracle's cheeks at her daughter's pain and her own torment and crusted into lines of salt threatened to spill over once more. Her heart skipped, pulse thundering. She should have known her torment was far from over, should have known the Sorceress could never resist—

"What of it?" her daughter shot back, brushing her long braid off her shoulder.

"I cannot allow you entry into the Pentacle until I

know it has been carried out. Such a step would disrespect the other three Faces and myself."

Her daughter's hands tightened into fists. Was her child prepared to do what the Sorceress was suggesting? "The ceremony is performed after the former Oracle passes on." Her voice warbled. It was a mistake to show fear in the face of one such as the Sorceress. Such a misstep heightened her already inflated sense of herself, invited further cruelties.

This was her punishment for watching the torment the Sorceress put the alchemists and their families through, that she would put the offerings through after the elements were distilled.

"That is the normal way of things, it is true," the Sorceress admitted.

The Oracle wasn't sure whether to be more disappointed in her daughter or herself. The Sorceress was too steady in her ambition and unpredictability for either of them to have underestimated her, for her to be acting against their line of succession, threatening the passage of their magic in this way. She endangered an entire sect of mages not to mention the memory of their line and the prophecies they had inherited and been charged to see through into being.

"But we are not in normal circumstances, as you're well aware," the Sorceress murmured. "You have enacted a coup. And so the task falls to you to see through the magical transference you began." She gestured to a side table the Oracle hadn't noted before. On it was a scalpel and a strangely shaped set of pliers, rounded.

Her stomach heaved.

Rounded very much like the shape of an eye.

For the first time since she'd been released from the torture chair where she'd been restrained, her daughter met her gaze.

Such a significant gesture, in most cases. How one gauged the measure of a person, part of how one understood one's place in the world.

The Oracle couldn't help but think that as her daughters' eyes met her own, the young elf before her was gazing into her next meal. Which eye would she devour first? She remembered having a similar debate about her mother's, while her advisers hovered in the edges of the room and her mother's aides and friends wept in the hallway outside.

She'd only been able to devour the one without retching.

The Sorceress would never allow such restraint, she realized. Her daughter would pluck them both out and devour them while her mother screamed in agony or fainted in shock.

She would awaken in a dungeon, with both her physical sight and her magical gifting from her ancestors removed.

The Oracle wasn't sure which was more cruel.

"As you're ready," the Sorceress said to the Oracle's daughter.

The girl's lip trembled, and then she slid toward the implements.

So the betrayal truly begins, the Oracle thought to herself, remembering the warning from the broken phoenix figure.

She could only hope that, had they succeeded in recalling the phoenix soul back to Eldura, the phoenix would be more skilled at avoiding the schemes of the Sorceress and the soon-to-be Oracle than she had been.

The Oracle stared down her daughter as she approached, refusing to offer a word of comfort or, for the Sorceress, a glimmer of fear beyond what her body could not suppress.

There would be time for all of that later.

A final vision flashed with certainty across her mind, a last gifting of Sight before all she had was stripped away by the very being she'd carried and brought into this world.

A flaming phoenix descended upon a druid conclave in the deep forest. A sweaty brow of garnet hair. Loving, bright green eyes gazing down.

A baby, cradled in her parents' arms, her elf ears still pink from birth.

The phoenix looked up from the glowing rafters above the family. It thrust itself up into the air, pirouetted, and plunged toward the baby.

The mystical bird condensed as it fell, shrinking itself in size until it matched the baby before rippling over and then sinking into the child's chest.

A soft coo—bird and baby as one—echoed out from between the exhausted parents.

As they'd hoped for, Lilia had returned.

And the magical promise of Verdigris, a being who could bear the six elements, united as one, had been renewed.

CHAPTER SEVEN

THE SORCERESS

THREE MONTHS LATER

"**A**re you ready?" The Sorceress stared down her nose at the new Oracle who was settling into her role. She should have intervened sooner, should have seen through the girl's mother's entreaties of alliance. It remained uncertain if there were lingering consequences of the Oracle's betrayal that had not yet appeared.

"I am," the new Oracle answered, falling into step alongside the Sorceress as they strolled down the dungeon halls toward a newly renovated dungeon wing set up specifically for the next phase of her Hexblade experiments.

She did admire the gravitas of the treachery. In the aftermath of the passage of the Oracle's line from mother to daughter, the Sorceress's guards had subdued those of the other Face and granted the Sorceress the time she needed to parse through the Oracle's correspondence.

One of the Oracle's agents had burned the Oracle's records.

The Sorceress had seen her burned in turn. Slowly.

There was no way of knowing what had been lost in the hearth filled with documents, but what she *had* gleaned filled her with a greater respect for the one she'd seen removed from her position of power.

The one who lay locked away and forgotten within her dungeons still.

Though the Oracle's scheme lacked the theater of her own treachery, she couldn't deny the intrigue of the stakes the Oracle had risked her life and others' for. A return of a granddaughter of Verdigris—Lilia, one whom the Oracle believed stood the best chance of uniting the six elements.

No wonder Yvayne had been so eager to intervene.

They were about to see whether such sacrifice had been necessary.

In her own eagerness to dispose of the Oracle and see a more pliable Oracle slated into place, she had neglected a few aspects of her questioning, a mistake she did not plan to make again.

The Oracle had confessed to her treaties from the outer conclaves and an arrangement with Yvayne. But there was still something missing. Aside from the shared aim of uniting the elements, the only addition the Sorceress could imagine the revived soul offering the Hexblade experiments was that Lilia's natural giftings would offer a stabilization of the elements, a boon she wished she'd imagined herself as it could be a great help.

There was no need to wait for such a success though.

If the distillation of the Cities' alchemists' elemental magic could be imbued into the flesh of an offering, they might not even need the stabilizing force of a returned soul.

How the Oracle had sought to return this soul remained a mystery, as did the question of whether or not she had been successful.

The experiments with the offerings had moved apace, as had the elemental distillery, once she'd gotten the alchemists in line.

Several of their family members had served in her initial test runs of the elemental offerings, as had her own guards. A necessary cost in magical experimentation, and one that had made the others far more pliable to her demands.

"What precisely should we be expecting during this phase of the trials?" the new Oracle asked, unable to suppress the quaver from her voice.

"Our initial imbuing of most of the elements into either a willing host or an offering have been a success, but the presence of a single element is far from what is needed for the creation of a true Hexblade."

"You need the six," the new Oracle answered.

"Precisely."

Guards and mages bowed to the pair of them as they crossed the dungeon hallways. She had the passageway redone with alternating lanterns made from the distilled elements, giving the hallway the feeling of dwelling within a cursed rainbow.

"There is a danger to the experiment," the Sorceress

added. "Are you sure you are ready to witness the next phase of our Hexblade creation?"

Rebellion flared in the new Oracle's eyes, one of which glowed with familiar strands of silver—the remnants of her mother's Sight, visible only to those who knew to look for it. "Of course I am."

"Well enough." The Sorceress gestured for the younger Face to enter the chamber ahead of her. If the girl was bothered by her return to the site where they'd trapped and tricked her mother, she showed no indication of such.

With half the captured alchemists and their families dead and the others waiting in cells to serve as offerings, the Sorceress had seen the grand experiment chambers broken up into a smaller series of rooms with a secret hallway that led out of the tower in case of an explosive emergency. The distilled elements were unruly, almost as unwieldy as the Sorceress herself. She wasn't taking any chances in her own survival, but she *would* bring the titans' might to heel.

She'd arranged for the next phase of their experiment already. Her guards had carefully observed and collected the most promising of the offerings—those who had best bonded with their first elements—and this experiment would see them add the second.

She'd carefully read through the files of all the offerings. Those who had selected the element of fire had each died out, which suggested that Ignis's magic might prove the most difficult to wield. A slight miscalculation on her part had brought about the death of at least one family member for each of the fire alchemists who were proving to be equally difficult in and of themselves. She had to play her hand with care to ensure the survival of her experiment.

Five offerings had been selected for this next phase, starting with the best of the offerings to water, and she'd also appointed the best of her elemental imbuers for the task, a merchild named Sethavian.

"We are ready when you are, Sorceress," her chief apprentice told her, gesturing to the collection of offerings along one wall, the nervous imbuer and his tutor, and the gaggle of waiting adepts who would lend whatever aid the Sorceress commanded.

"Excellent," the Sorceress answered. She straightened, easily stretching into full command of the room. At her gesture, the Oracle peeled away from her side and positioned herself along the far wall, out of the way by the door. The experiment would take her full attention, and she couldn't risk the new Oracle distracting her from this important next step.

"You are each privy to a profound moment in the history of Lis-Maen and the united might of the Pentacle," the Sorceress began, addressing those gathered. Her mages and guards were the only ones who shifted in their expression at the Sorceress's grandiose claims, but aside from Sethavian and perhaps the Oracle, the others mattered little in the grander scheme beyond the current phase. "Should this next stage of our experiment succeed, we will be that much closer to a reclamation of the elemental magics stolen from our borders by the Cities, a wrong we seek this very day to right."

A smattering of polite applause answered her declaration. One of the offerings coughed wetly in the corner.

"But enough preamble," the Sorceress said. Her desire for pomp had faded with her growing awareness of the prickles of magic in the room and the chance to tame the elements by their combining.

On their own, an elemental warrior sworn to a single element could do little beyond match the champions and their dedication to the Cities. But with the elements combined, the Cities United would have no answer. They would have but one choice—bending the knee to her superior magic and might.

"The element of fire, if you please." She beckoned the strongest of the offerings forward, an elf imbued with the element of water, selected from the slums of Delmoir, just outside the academy's grounds. Beads of sweat clung to his brow, and he had struggled to keep down food since their imbuing of water.

The Healer's apprentices told her the offering's body was beginning to bloat. If they were to take full advantage of their test, there was no better time.

"Sethavian," she called, waving the merchild forward as well. He'd been entrusted as a peace offering to the Pentacle on behalf of the rulers of Nepta and given the ability to dwell upon land. In exchange for their promise of mutual cooperation and alliance, he would be the mercourt's eyes and ears upon the surface.

The Sorceress had perceived his greater promise almost immediately, one with a natural aptitude for channeling the elements. "Have you prepared?" she asked the boy. To those who weren't aware of his heritage, he would appear like any other elf on the verge of entering adulthood. It was only the azure of his eyes, flecked with sapphire rather than copper or gold, that truly gave his origins away.

He bowed his head. "Y-yes, Sorceress. Only—"

"Go on."

The boy wetted his lips. "The fire is more an approximation, the alchemists warned me. Their original supply isn't pure like air and earth." He glanced at the sweating offering. "They aren't sure what the impact of its mixed nature might be. Th-that's why they l-lost the first offerings."

At this revelation, the subdued offering to water straightened, looking down in alarm at the child. From the edge of the chamber, the new Oracle directed one of the guards forward to help reassure and subdue the offering. It wouldn't do to upset Sethavian. He was too valuable to their project. Perhaps the new Oracle would be as useful as the Sorceress had hoped when she'd begun recruiting the girl to her cause years ago.

"Ah." The Sorceress raised her hands and pushed back her sleeves, stooping slightly to stare into the boy's eyes. "That is *precisely* why we perform experiments, is it not?" Her grin widened. "If we left it to the experimenters, elemental alchemy and mechanomancy would remain matters only explored in books." She clicked her tongue behind her teeth. "*We* are among those brave enough to see what's truly possible."

The offering in the corner coughed wetly, ruining the ending of her speech.

The Sorceress glared at the offender. "Proceed when

you are ready, Sethavian." She strode away so she could keep the whole of the room beneath her surveillance.

With the help of one of his tutors, the boy stood before the cart with needle, vial, and a glass beaker of glimmering fire. A specialist had been summoned from among the Creatrix's apprentices to help handle the flames, the most volatile element of the six for all save Ignis's champions of fire.

The apprentice held the corked vial of bottled flame out toward Sethavian who inserted the needle inside, withdrawing a thin stream of molten flame into the contraption a previous set of captured alchemists had devised under the Sorceress's supervision before they'd all expired a few years before.

She held her breath.

The boy approached the offering's side. Another aide had already rolled up the man's sleeve and laid him back against the table. They strapped him down for good measure.

In another room along this corridor, the offerings who were struggling with the elements were lending themselves to another iteration of her plan. Mages with a complementary magic to Seth's were extracting the elements from the offerings' bodies to see what effects came about within the elements themselves.

Invariably, the removal killed the struggling hosts, but the next round of offerings who were bound within the rooms to receive the doubly distilled elements were taking to their first imbuings well.

Such sacrifices were necessary for the creation of her elemental warriors. Those who could rival the might of the champions—taking on the six like Verdigris, yes. But also like the dark goddess when she defeated the other first champions and ascended into godhood.

After the Oracle's encouragement, the boy swallowed hard, and his tutor encouraged him forward again, speaking softly to him.

With a deep breath, Sethavian began his imbuing. His brow furrowed and lower lip protruded slightly in his concentration.

The offering winced when the needle met his skin. With great effort, he forced his eyes shut.

The Sorceress scanned his body, waiting for some sign that the magic was either working or had failed.

Steam began to rise from the elf's skin.

She pressed her nails into her palms.

The offering tightened his jaw, clenched his fists. He groaned out a muffled cry. The steam grew thicker.

"Get him back," the Sorceress commanded Sethavian's tutor, sensing the yawning pulse of magic gathering in the air.

The tutor did as she bid just in time.

With a piercing scream, the offering reared back, thrashing against his bindings.

Starting from Seth's tattooed markings, the offering's skin caught fire. His clothing quickly followed.

The Sorceress darted toward the tutor and the boy and guided them out into the hall, the new Oracle rushing out just behind her. The Sorceress's guards poured into the room, ready to subdue the body should the burning offering break free.

A disappointing loss.

"Get Sethavian back to his room," she ordered the tutor. "If he needs a memory alteration to recover, alert me at once."

"Yes, mistress." The tutor bowed and ushered the shaking boy away.

The rest was over within the hour—the room cleansed, the body disposed of, the Oracle sent back to her tower with plans to review their notes in a few days.

The Sorceress stood alone in the chamber after the last traces of ash had been removed, though the scent of smoke and flesh still lingered.

When conducting experiments, it was important to be as objective as possible, particularly to not allow what one wished to have happened to cause one to stray in one's observation of what had actually occurred.

A single, objective truth hovered alongside the foul odors in the room, landing like twin ravens upon the Sorceress's shoulders. The element of fire was going to challenge her plans. But she had never been one to accept defeat.

The stakes were too high for the future of Lis-Maen, for their independence from the Cities and for her own determination of whatever future she most wanted for herself and those under her power.

An alliance with Alessandra, if she wished.

Or to become like the dark goddess herself, an army imbued with the elements ready to answer her every command.

The fire would be brought to heel like every other foe she'd ever faced. And with her own elemental army, no one would stand in her way.

CHAPTER EIGHT
ANDEUS

"That's it, Kailena," Andeus soothed, tears pricking at the corners of his eyes. He wiped the sweat from Kailena's brow, careful to remain out of the way of the healers who had gathered for the birth of their child.

For days now, his partner had run a fever that the healers struggled to subdue. They thought it might prove to be a complication with the birth. Kailena held Andeus's gaze in those moments, begging him to keep quiet.

It was a complication.

A magical cost that would take the person he loved most, leaving him to raise their daughter alone.

Yvayne could not help him, not for some time. She had withdrawn again after an accident in the Emeraude but not before she warned them away from a coup at the Pentacle, the death of the Oracle they knew, their friend.

The first in the blood cost of Lilia's return.

Twin crescent moons hovered high overhead, occasionally reflecting in the fever-brightness of Kailena's glazed eyes. "We did it, Andeus," she murmured to him over and over again. "I can feel it."

Andeus swallowed his tears, condensing them into a knot in his chest that would yawn open, never to close, when his partner departed this plane.

He grasped her hand in his, savoring her scent, her closeness, every detail he could before the end, whenever it would come.

THE PHOENIX

High above the young family that was about to be, a spectral baby phoenix descended, sent away from Astralei—she wasn't quite sure why.

Fire and earth she knew to look for.

Flaming red hair and bright green eyes were what she found.

With a grunt and a cry, a tiny, blood-covered elven baby emerged into the world.

Though her hair was matted and eyes squinted shut, the phoenix knew this was the one she'd been sent to.

Her match.

The phoenix's instincts took over, sending her up into the sky before plunging down as Andeus marveled overhead at the fiery streak of a comet rushing by, crossing the paths of the twin dark moons.

The phoenix shrank herself down, condensing to the size of the child's heart so they might grow as one, separate and together, like the soul she'd bound herself to before, the soul she'd been sent to find again.

As the phoenix settled into the child's heartspace, she tried to remember the life she'd known before, the soul who had saved her, who she needed to be reunited with for the world to be made whole.

But such a quest made little sense with the coziness of a family circled about her, the baby—herself—cradled between the two parents and held close.

"Welcome to Eldura, Rowan," the woman whispered.

"We love you, little one," the father added, pressing a kiss to the woman's brow. "Rest now, both of you, and I'll keep watch."

The phoenix curled tighter around Rowan's heart, soothed by the promise of protection.

When the time came, she could offer the same safety to the heart she'd found, the heart that was her and hers.

YVAYNE

Deep within the Emeraude, Yvayne sat back from her scrying bowl with a sigh, crossing herself with the sign of the six and lighting a candle to each of the titans in turn.

Her hand shook as she lit the seventh candle at the middle of the elemental structure—six candles for the elements, five branches for the natural magics. For the first time in millennia, she lit the candle of Verdigris, welcoming one of the titan's granddaughters back into the world.

Yvayne sighed and wiped at the corner of her eyes as she turned away from the candle, running her fingertips absentmindedly over the sachet of protection she wore around her neck including a talisman the Oracle had sent her before her demise.

As they'd hoped for, Lilia had returned.

And the magical promise of Verdigris, a being who could bear the six elements, united as one, had been renewed.

"Wherever you go," Yvayne whispered over the sachet, her way of communing with the child, "you will carry fire, water, earth, light, darkness, and air. No others know what it is to possess the six united. Your magic is renewed, revived, a spark of Verdigris.

"And with your birth returns her promise: From the ashes I rise." Yvayne narrowed her eyes, staring out beyond the library cave, imagining glaring into the eyes of her enemy through the ages, Alessandra, the one who had overseen the destruction of her homeland and was trying to dismantle this world in turn. "So may it be done."

***

FOLLOW ALONG AS THE SPARK OF VERDIGRIS CATCHES INTO FLAME!

Thank you so much for reading *Hexblade*, the prequel novella for the *Feather & Flame* dark fantasy epic!

Rowan's journey begins in *Phoenix Rising*, book one in the series. You'll find more of the intricate schemes, intense sacrifices, and epic magic of *Hexblade* in *Phoenix Rising*!

Rowan knows what she must do: Harness her elemental magic, revive a lost titan, and restore the ebbing might of her forest home.

But to increase her power, she must ally herself with long-standing enemies, those responsible for her father's death and the weakening of the woods.

And she's not the only one to face the scant choices of a world at war.

Across the Circle Sea, Marcon prepares for his first deployment as a soldier in the Army of Light, led by the famed Tali Silversword, one of the last remaining elemental champions. They return to Sanctuary, the battleground that claimed his parents' lives years before.

Alongside Rowan and Marcon, the threads of fate intertwine a dwarf desperate for redemption, an elf searching for his sister, and a nameless spirit witch fighting to survive.

Explore a world of fading elemental magic, secret heroes, and brimming war in this enthralling first-in-series dark fantasy epic with themes of destiny, found family, and inner power.

JOURNEY DEEPER INTO ELDURA

For behind-the-scenes updates, fantasy map deep-dives, and all the latest happenings in Eldura, visit bethball books.com/join to be part of my newsletter community, the Circle of Story.

And finally, for signed copies, (upcoming) special editions, and art prints, visit bethballbooks.shop.

RENEWED, REVIVED, A SPARK OF VERDIGRIS

The war for Eldura is only just beginning.

In book one of the *Feather & Flame* dark fantasy epic, Rowan, the one who carries the phoenix, departs from her home in Willow Glen to face her enemies and grow her magic.

The series continues with *From the Ashes*, book two.

THE FLAME BURNS ANEW

If you love the epic stakes, intricate magic systems, fascinating villains, and inspiring heroines of the *Feather & Flame* series, answer the call of adventure in Beth's *Age of Azuria* epic fantasy series, featuring Yvayne at a much later point in her career as an adventurer's guide.

Your journey begins in "Awakened Flame," a crossover story from the world of Eldura to Azuria, starring one of the heroes from *Phoenix Rising*, a soldier in the Army of Light, Marcon Colabra.

The battle for an age begins more simply than one might think—an elven diplomat, a human noble-woman, and the forbidden love that would change their world, forever.

Elven diplomat Dorric Themear has experienced the giddy flutterings of new love before. But not like this. Behind the sapphire eyes of Lady Emelyee Amastacia lies a long-awaited destiny that neither of them can sense or stop.

However, forces darker than Emelyee's husband are prepared to stand in their way.

Close on the couple's heels, Ridel, one of Lucien's most trusted servants, is less than enthused about her assignment to watch the would-be lovers. If only her master had been visionary enough to see that a child cannot result if the parents are dead. She'll do her best to comply with his orders to observe and to wait—at least for now.

Although Dorric and Emelyee do not suspect the role they play in the larger story of Azuria, they have a secret protector lingering in the shadows, preparing for precisely this moment. High in the Frostmaw Mountains, Yvayne has seen the signs of the turning of the age before. This time, with the proper intervention, she and the druids can make their play for Azuria.

In this prequel novella for the *Age of Azuria* high fantasy series, competing forces converge in a battle for the future of their world—a future that hangs upon the return of a long-awaited soul. And, of course, on Dorric's ability to woo the human noblewoman whose affections lie beyond his reach.

Visit bethballbooks.com/aurora to join Beth's reading community, and you'll receive a free copy of *Aurora*, the prequel novella for the *Age of Azuria* series.

There are worlds of adventure waiting for you across the Storyverse!

ABOUT THE AUTHOR

Beth Ball is a weaver of words and worlds spinning stories of druidic magic and the power of nature that span the epic fantasy realms of Eldura, Azuria, and beyond. If you enjoy lyrical tales of action and adventure, dragons, werewolves, fae, wily foxes, and more, then grab your enchanted amulet, flaming longsword, poisoned dagger, or other mystical accessory of choice, and let's start our adventure!

You can find more of Beth's work and the legends of Eldura at bethballbooks.com. And if you're looking for playable, immersive adventures in Beth's Storyverse, visit groveguardianpress.com.

GLOSSARY

WORLDS & PLANES

Planes of Life, *three interconnected planes*, Eldura, Shadowlands, and Brightlands
Astralei, spirit plane

ELEMENTAL TITANS

Ignis, titan of fire
Atamos, titan of air
Ilona, titan of light
Gaia, titan of earth
Thalyssa, titan of water

Nyx, titan of darkness
Verdigris, titan of nature, *destroyed and transformed into the three planes of life*
Izadra, titan of space, *destroyed and transformed into the spirit plane, Astralei*

POLITICAL POWERS AND ORGANIZATIONS OF ELDURA

Alessandra, the dark goddess, power centralized in **Scourge**
Cities United – Respite, Beacon, Sanctuary, Palais, Vestige, Bastion, Verita
The Five Faces of the Pentacle – Sorceress, Oracle, Creatrix, Druidess, Healer; figureheads of the Academia Magica and rulers of the recently centralized peoples of Lis-Maen, including the various druid conclaves
The Witches of the Emeraude – collected into covens, each ruled by a grand matron
Unaffiliated peoples of the **Glade of Shadows**, including the Sapphire Circle (powerful druid conclave) and the dryads

Champions, elemental warriors appointed by the titans who serve the Cities United
Lorekeepers – collective of secret keepers who slip between borders to preserve the lore, magic, and history of Eldura
Order of Verdigris – a secret organization founded by

Lilith dedicated to restoring Verdigris and her will upon the planes of life; closely aligned with the lorekeepers

DEITIES

Alessandra, "the dark goddess," goddess of negation
Cassandra, goddess of fate, patron deity of the saudad (travelers)
Lilith, demigoddess and revolutionary figure for the Shadowlands fae, daughter of Arrakis (goddess of spiders) and Nyx

FOLKLORIC HEROES

Hugh & Lilia, a Lycan and a fae, respectively; heroes before the Fall of the First Age who sacrificed their love to save their peoples
Daughters of Verdigris, Evelyn (mother of the Shadowlands fae, sometimes referred to as lummenfae or Umbral fae) and grandmother of Yvayne, Enid (mother of the Brightlands fae, sometimes referred to as brightfae) and mother of Lilia, Lyric (mother of druids whose magic transferred to the prime plane)
Ravenna, deposed queen of the Shadowlands who now shelters in hiding; mother of Yvayne